ɑ
Conviviality

Other titles in the Hodder African Readers series

The Fearless Four	978 0340 940426
The Fearless Four: Hijack!	978 0340 940419
The Fearless Four and the Graveyard Ghost	978 0340 940358
The Fearless Four and the Smugglers	978 0340 940334
Dead Men's Bones	978 0340 940365
Twin Trouble	978 0340 940310
Sauna and the Drug Pedlars	978 0340 940402
The Power of Corruption	978 0340 940341
Magic, Mystery and Mister Prince	978 0340 940389
Time Bomb	978 0340 940327
God's Case: No Appeal	978 0340 940372
One Man, Two Votes	978 0340 940396
Dear Miss Winfrey	978 0340 984178
Shoot for the Moon	978 0340 984215
Madulo & Co.	978 0340 984185
The Button Bottle	978 0340 984222
The Mystery of Rukodzi Mountain	978 0340 984239
A Few Little Lies	978 0340 984154
Secret Celebrity	978 0340 984208
No More Secrets	978 0340 984192

Conquest & Conviviality

By Tolu Ogunlesi

Illustrated by Andrew Mokgatla

AN HACHETTE UK COMPANY

Hachette UK's policy is to use papers that are natural, renewable
and recyclable products and made from wood grown in sustainable
forests. The logging and manufacturing processes are expected to
conform to the environmental regulations of the country of origin.

Orders: please contact Bookpoint Ltd, 130 Milton Park, Abingdon, Oxon
OX14 4SB. Telephone: (44) 01235 827720. Fax: (44) 01235 400454. Lines
are open 9.00–5.00, Monday to Saturday, with a 24-hour message
answering service. Visit our website at www.hoddereducation.co.uk

© Tolu Ogunlesi 2008
First published in 2008 by
Hodder Education,
An Hachette UK Company
338 Euston Road
London NW1 3BH

Impression number   5 4 3 2
Year   2012 2011

All rights reserved. Apart from any use permitted under UK copyright law,
no part of this publication may be reproduced or transmitted in any form
or by any means, electronic or mechanical, including photocopying and
recording, or held within any information storage and retrieval system,
without permission in writing from the publisher or under licence from
the Copyright Licensing Agency Limited. Further details of such licences
(for reprographic reproduction) may be obtained from the Copyright
Licensing Agency Limited, Saffron House, 6-10 Kirby Street, London EC1N 8TS.

Cover and illustrations by Andrew Mokgatla
Typeset in 13/16 Bembo by RockBottom g&d, KZN, SA
Printed in Great Britain by CPI Cox & Wyman, Reading, RG1 8EX

A catalogue record for this title is available from the British Library

ISBN 978 0340 984161

*To every parent who has ever dreamt on behalf of a child,
And to every child with dreams of his or her own.*

PART ONE

My life is headed downhill, and I've pawned my brakes

I wasn't even informed of the decision of the panel beforehand. The news was broken to the entire school on the assembly ground, on a day I remembered to attend. It was a very cruel way to do it, if you ask me. Later I heard the panel was split equally between those who wanted me expelled, and those who wanted me suspended for two weeks. So the one-term suspension was a compromise, a cross between two misguided decisions.

It was supposed to be WITH IMMEDIATE EFFECT. No chance to do anything but pack my things. I didn't even have the chance to check my secret traps on the outskirts of the school farms, the traps I hoped would catch the Agriculture Tutor. But they did me one little kindness – the school that is. They put me in a taxi and instructed the driver to take me home. Must have cost a fortune.

So that was how I left St Gregory's College, Lagos, on a forced, three-month vacation, clutching a letter that was addressed 'TO WHOM IT MAY CONCERN' (as if I didn't have a Mother) stating my crimes against humanity, and expressing the hope and desire that I would return reformed. Tsk!

When we got into Lagos I managed to beg the driver of the car to allow me stop at the post office. Told him my cancer-stricken father, long divorced from my mother, had asked me please to write him a letter every week.

What I wanted to mail was my 'death sentence' letter. The last thing I was going to do was hand it over to Mother with my own hands. God forbid a bad thing. I was going to drop it in the post office for her, and inform her that the school had mailed it. I was sure that she wouldn't take note of the stamp date in the excitement of the contents.

Ground Rules

Some ground rules about me before we go on:

1. I do not believe in friends, pals, companions, buddies, allies, associates, comrades, or whatever name they come by. So I have none, and do not want any. Alone we come into the world, and alone we shall make our way through. Trying to carry on through life with a band of fellow humans is pointless.
2. I hate my twin sister (full name Conviviality; Convive for short).
3. My twin sister doesn't like me (much).
4. I have a mother who doesn't think much of me.
5. I have a mother who doesn't know how wide the gap is between my sister and I.
6. The relationship between my sister and I is made up largely of 'episodes' in which we try to outdo each other in unkindness.
7. You will learn the other Rules as we go.

Uphill

By contrast, my twin sister's life is headed uphill, at TOP speed, in sixth gear.

Convive has just returned from Europe. Yes, Europe. She was holed up in some Swiss or Swedish (I confuse the two) castle or something, for two weeks, her prize for coming third in the National Mathematical Competition. She called Mother every other day from there. Not once did she ask to speak to me. Not once did Mother ask her if she wanted to.

The Fugitive

Right now I'm a busy man. Busy dodging Mother, even though we live in the same house. I can't stand the way she eyes me like I'm some new improved brand of failure. Like she should have taken me for an IQ test before adopting me. Of course I ignore her, or simply eye her back to let her know she should have been smart enough to leave me behind in the orphanage from which I came. After all, she's got Convive. One promising child is enough in the family.

I'm also busy doing other things. Learning to smoke cigars, for instance. It's not the easiest thing in the world, and is not like smoking a cigarette. For one, cigars are rare, not available for easy practice like cigarettes.

Needless to say, Mother was mad when I arrived at home bearing news of the suspension of my academic career.

Not that she went mentally unstable. What I mean is she was mad *at me*. But there was a limit to which she could be mad at me now, because all my life I have made her mad at me. She threw up her hands in despair and wondered aloud (again) why she had made the mistake of adopting me. This was not a very kind thing to say aloud, but I'm not sure I can blame her. The truth is, anyone would feel that way; that, if an adopted child was going to bring so much trouble, then perhaps they should have left him to rot in the orphanage.

She cut off my pocket money and attempted to ground me, making me stay in the house. But she had to let me be, for the sake of peace. So the embargo on outings was lifted, but my accounts remained frozen.

I decided to look at my options. Going back to school was out of it. Instead, I was going to shame every one of my detractors. Now that they have chased me out of school, it looks like they have set me free.

By the time I finished work on the sheet of paper that showed my future, it looked something like this:

OPTIONS
Soccer; Professional; Local; Foreign; Agent
Suicide
America

Nothing much. But then I've come through life not expecting very much from life or fate.

Soccer
I have never stopped dreaming that one day I'll hit it big as a soccer star. It's not boasting, but I think I'm a pretty good soccer player. It's the only thing that gives me anything slightly resembling a sense of purpose. But of course, at school I hardly ever played football. The punishment for my misdeeds was exclusion from the soccer team. But what do I care? The soccer team is in the tight grip of a clique – a clique of congenital idiots. I play at home though – and did well last season. Well enough, though?

Suicide
Fact: In Germany I hear suicide is the second-leading cause of death in young people between the ages of 15 and 24, after road traffic accidents. It is therefore ruled out of my list. Why would I want to act like every other teenager?

America
America I hail thee! The land of Michael Jackson, O.J. Simpson, Michael Jordan, 50 cents, Elvis and J.F. Kennedy; the land of the Statue of Liberty; the land of Abraham Lincoln.

There is a dream I am always having – that I become the Crown Prince of a Kingdom whose capital is called 'Miami'. And I have a crown studded with 51 diamond stars. And every time I start to ask: 'What is the name of this Kingdom?' I find myself awake.

An episode (1)

I try sneaking into the house through the back door. I reckon Convive will be stuck in front of the TV watching *Super Story* or one of those Mexican soaps she is addicted to. When she is doing that, not even the Apocalypse will rouse her.

I am right *and* wrong. She *is* watching *Super Story* – and watching out for me at the same time. So as the back door swings open in slow motion, Convive's bat-woman ears are apparently also swinging open. She stands at the kitchen door, watching me and watching *Super Story* at the same time.

'Where have you been?'

I ignore her. She stands in my way, sniffing. 'You have been out with your gang again, eh?' she says, imitating her favorite Nollywood actress. I remain silent. It is all I can do to make sure she doesn't smell the two bottles of Gulder I have tossed back this evening. I attempt to push my way past her.

'Look at the time.' She switches to Mother's voice here. Convive is an excellent mimic. It drives me crazy. 'Is this the way you want to continue living your life, until you end up on the streets?'

The way she's talking I conclude Mother isn't home, and breathe out deeply in relief. I am not ready to do any explaining, or to listen to any sermon on how I have refused to count myself lucky to have such a privileged life, considering...

Considering what? Privileged life my foot!

I leave Convive to her act and head towards the pot of soup on the cooker, aiming to distract Convive that way. I succeed. As I lift the lid Convive hurls herself at me. Seconds later Convive and I are standing in a pool of soup, and staring glumly at the scattered chunks of chicken on the kitchen floor.

'See what you've done, you idiot?' she yells.

Mother will be back any time, and will be mad, and will of course believe that I did it. And I shall be convicted and sentenced accordingly. Normally I shouldn't be bothered, of course, but then, with the beer, I'm no longer thinking straight.

I stare at the mess as if I am some war general surveying the fallout of a recent battle.

I am going to have to cook new soup. Ten minutes later I am standing at the Odedinas' – our neighbours – kitchen window, receiving a donation of soup ingredients from their Nkechi, their house-girl, who apparently likes me, and will do anything I ask her to. The Odedinas are an elderly couple, whose children all live in America, and who live in the giant duplex next to ours and stock their kitchen as though they are anticipating a war some time soon. I knew that I was going to get enough ingredients to cook another pot of soup from their kitchen. Nkechi gives me all I need.

But of course there is still a problem. I cannot cook. Big deal. Convive will NOT help me out. Obviously she is hoping Mother will return and catch me in the middle of the mess.

Even though I cannot cook, I still go ahead and cook. And somehow, magically, miraculously, Mother cannot tell that the soup has changed. Even Convive is surprised.

In the Beginning

Convive and I didn't just drop from Mars, just like that. I am an adopted child. And so is my sister.

What I am about to tell you, we heard from our mother on the day we were 11. She was going to tell us on our twenty-first birthday, but she changed her mind and decided to fast-forward ten years because of a TV show she saw. On the show, an American woman, convicted of the murder of her husband, claimed that her mother hiding the fact that she was an adopted child had ruined her life. Not by the fact that she was adopted, but that her mother had kept that fact secret all her life. She had stumbled on it by mistake, and that was the beginning of the end for her.

So, since our Mother did not want us to become murderers/serial killers in the future, she sat us down on our eleventh birthday and gave us the news. I like to think it was her birthday gift to us that day.

I am not Convive, but I think I can say that our lives started to fall apart that day. And *we* started to fall apart, not because we were adopted – we could cope with that – but because we had been made to believe that we were real twins. Mother had told us these absolutely amazing and fantastic tales about how we had been born, how I had come out of her holding on tight to Convive's heels, with a smirk on my face. And how I had weighed almost double what Convive weighed. And how...

Now she confessed to us that she had made those stories up, and that she was sorry, and that we were adopted, and that we were not even real siblings, not to talk of being twins. And she pleaded with us to forgive her, and understand that she wanted the best for us. Which was why she had told us those happy stories. And that it was the TV show, something like a *Jerry Springer*, that made her realise the mistake she had made all along, keeping the truth from us.

And this, dear friends, is that *Truth*.

The Truth

I, Conquest, was one year old when my adventures as an unclaimed kid came to an end, and the plan of a future outside the Little Saints Orphanage, in Alagomeji, was signed, sealed and delivered to me.

Discounting the fact that I was very slightly underweight for my age, and that my right thumb almost permanently lived in my mouth, I think I qualified to be called cute.

The woman who adopted us had been a Mrs five whole years, childless, and her husband – 'Second Dad' – had acquired two wives after her. Eventually he abandoned her. Then she met another man, 'Third Dad' – forgive me, but I will have to use this crazy numbering system to make myself absolutely clear at all times – a widowed, childless man, four years younger, and together they adopted me. And together they bestowed on me my present name: Conquest. I hear I used to be Olusegun.

Ngozi, my so-called 'twin' sister, came to my mother's attention a year later. There was a news item on *NewsLine* about a two-year-old inmate of the Cheshire Motherless Babies' Home in Ibadan whose teenage mother (who had also grown up in the Home) had died minutes after giving birth to her. Mum, struck by the fact that Ngozi was born on the second of November ('the same day our Conquest was born'), dashed to the telephone and called the Home to ask if she could adopt the little girl.

That was the beginning of my New Sister. She was renamed Conviviality – Convive for short. Since she had been born eleven minutes before me she had to become my *big* twin sister. Her birth certificate said 1:23 a.m. Mine 1:34 a.m.

I can't remember when it was that I looked up the word 'Conviviality' in the *Oxford Advanced Learner's Dictionary*.

Convivial / adj. Cheerful and friendly in atmosphere or character.

I've never bothered to look up 'Conquest'.

As for our mother, you can get most of what you need to know about her from *our* story. She is a woman who has not been particularly fortunate with *The Opposite Sex*.

Two husbands who were in the past tense, and a string of nearly-husbands (this part Convive and I witnessed). But now it seems that she has given up on the sons of men, and has decided to take God as her husband. She is now a very respected member of our church, the Appointed Gospel Church of the Holy Trinity.

But every now and then she draws us into her private affairs and speaks of her regrets at never succeeding at the game of love.

And if there is something that she has very perfectly passed down to her offspring – adoption notwithstanding – it is this ill-luck with *The Opposite Sex*.

An episode (2)

We were 15 last November, Convive and I, and there was a party.

The idea of a party was not mine. It was Convive's. Of course, I knew she'd have far more guests than me. And her 37 birthday cards were obviously far more than my 7. But it was really no big deal to me. What use are cards, after all? It's only a girl who'd think of leaving them dangling, insides strewn with cobwebs, months after they have outlived their usefulness. I didn't want the party in the first place, so no one should blame me if I didn't have many guests.

Convive flicked her hair off her face like it was a scorpion – the way she does when she's just been afflicted with a brainwave, and suddenly said, very sarcastically, 'Let's bet who's going to get more presents.' I looked at her like she was going crazy.

'No. Not the number of gifts,' I heard myself say. 'The value. Let's bet who's going to get the most valuable, most expensive gift.'

She looked at me, as though to say, what's the difference, you idiot? And then she nodded. And I immediately kicked myself for giving in to her stupid bet. I shrugged, and murmured a quick prayer that she would forget the whole silly thing. The loser of the bet would forfeit a month's pocket money to the winner. I picked up a calendar to be sure how long a month would be. Thirty days, plus or minus one.

We posed for pictures in front of the cake and all the cards, Convive arranging hers to one side, leaving a discreet gap between hers and mine. Of course, I didn't feel any self-pity. But I was glad when the day vroomed to an end – until I remembered our bet.

Convive poured all her presents out on the sitting-room floor, in the middle of all the empty cans of Coca-Cola and bits of rice pressed neatly into the carpet. She had got gifts from her friends who flooded the whole house like a stormy sea, and did nothing but giggle annoyingly all day long. I had already started to prepare myself for a month of starvation.

Since, of course, I had no guests and almost no gifts.

But at the end of it all, to my surprise, and to the surprise of my thumping heart, I won the bet. At the last minute, after Convive had taunted me to her heart's content, and just as she was about to declare herself winner, a present sauntered in for me.

It came from my football coach. One of the few men in the world I think I respect. He's supposed to

be in Qatar now, coaching a Third Division Football Team. He got tired of Nigeria and ran away, literally. Like I might soon be forced to.

I hadn't told him about the party, but he said he had looked up my birth date in the records, for some form he had to fill in, and decided to surprise me. Well, I hate to boast, but, the truth is, I had done well under his coaching. I had a sure place on the starting 11. That was apart from being the Golden Boot runner-up for two consecutive seasons in the Yaba Neighbourhood Premiership. And a member (ex-Acting Captain in fact) of the winning team of the Lagos State Youth Soccer Championships. So I suppose that's why he went to the trouble of getting me a birthday present. I got a brand new pair of Adidas boots. Four thousand bucks on the market. Convive's most expensive gift was an ugly teddy bear.

One more thing about this stupid birthday affair

Our Uncle Barnard, who is the world's meanest, stingiest inhabitant, and also Mum's chronic-bachelor younger brother, gave us – as always – books for birthday gifts. Dr Convive the Merciful, the Teenage Mother-Theresa-with-a-Stethoscope, got a book titled *Medicine My Passport*, the memoirs of a Nigerian Professor of Medicine.

Conquest got a tome titled *How To Make the Most of Your Life!* Mean Uncle Barnard is apparently convinced, like many other people, that Conquest's life is headed nowhere – fast. As if I care.

I'm going to make the least possible out of my life. Or maybe I'm going to score 30 goals in a World Cup and then refuse the Golden Boot.

Convive has got a first-class ticket on the train to Surgeonistan. She doesn't hesitate to tell anyone who cares to listen, and they respond by looking at her ever so sweetly and urging her on, before instinctively turning to me with that menacing 'and-what-about-you?' gaze.

When they advance upon me with that look blazing from their eyes like machine-gun fire, I volley it back with an 'of-course-I'm-going-to-be-a-lawyer' declaration. My bulletproof vest.

A lawyer and a doctor. Conviviality Clinics and Conquest & Co (Barristers and Solicitors). The best combination any parent could possibly have.

The birthday before last, back when Uncle Barnard still retained some hope about the existence of a future for me, he gave me a crappy law book. It was filled with all sorts of arcane stuff: lawyers' language, lawyers' dry jokes, guidelines for bar exams and endless pages written in legalese like *Whereupon which aim is to conceal the nature of the aforementioned act*. That year Convive got Margaret Thatcher's biography. Autographed by Thatcher herself.

An episode (3)

Every afternoon, Mum compelled us to meditate upon books for an hour at least. To help us get inspired for our future professions, she explained. From where I sat – lay, actually – I watched Convive sink into hers, flipping the pages deliciously as she read each one, getting into the flow of the book.

As for me, I hated my book so much that at first I did nothing but wait (in vain) for my hour to succumb. Eventually I decided to while away my time counting the number of times 'whereupon' appeared in the book.

Then, all of a sudden, I heard my mouth creak open (I swear), slowly, as if it were a noisy door someone was trying to open without making a hell of a noise. I knew then that Something Bad was in the air. 'Hey, Convive, um, how many dads do you think we'd have had by the time we die?'

Convive stared at me like she didn't hear right, her mouth wriggled into a crazy shape, like there was a snake in there trying to prise itself out of captivity, and she began to cry, very, very quietly.

That was the last time I'd make her cry. No matter how much I tried after that.

But no one really wanted you

There is something else I remember, about another birthday. I think it was our twelfth. I tried to kill myself. And this is no joke. It was on that day that I got an anonymous birthday card that said:

HAPPY BIRTHDAY.
BUT NO ONE REALLY WANTED YOU.

What made it really painful was that I didn't know who had sent me the card. All I knew was that someone out there hated me that much. And knew so much about me. Though the truth is, all my life I have accumulated enemies. Right from kindergarten, I have tried to put people *in their place*. For a long time I suspected it was Convive, my sister, who sent that card. And I made sure she paid for it, even though I wasn't sure.

PART TWO

Convive Disappears

I think I want to be a politician instead of being a lawyer. I want to move around in convoys and spend half of my waking hours shaking hands with people and giving long boring speeches. And living big.

I am in my room practising Martin Luther King's famous speech (which, by the way, is neither long nor boring) when I hear a knock. The door opens slowly and Mother peeks in.

'Did your sister call you?' she asks, eyeing the humongous pile of dirty jeans on the floor near my bed.

'Convive?' I say, which is a stupid thing to say. Mother glares at me. 'No,' I add quickly. I've learnt to say only what I need to say when talking with Mother. Rule 213 in the *Conquest Compendium of Necessary Wisdom*. Use the least amount of words you can use. In the past I'd have told her when last I saw Convive, and where, and all of that. Now, 'I don't know' is all I say.

Mother's eyes shift to the plates stacked together on my desk. Two meals yesterday and today's breakfast. I am fidgety. But she doesn't say anything, the door slamming shut behind her. Seconds later I have left Mother and Convive and Nigeria behind, and am swaying in front of a crowd in far-away Alabama, showing crowds of teenagers visions of a future free from the tyranny of parents.

It is not until I come downstairs in search of something to eat that it dawns on me there is a problem. Mum is on the phone, pacing up and down, her voice unsteady. I stand behind the kitchen door eavesdropping. Whatever it is, it isn't good news. But Mother is great at concealing. She could be on the phone for eternity and you wouldn't be able to tell what she was talking about. But that's because she consciously throws in confusing details. (This is not surprising, not when her son is an unrepentant eavesdropper.)

Then she calls my name. One good look at her and I can tell that things are far from well. Her hands are trembling, her speech is trailing off, her mind is not with me. Convive is in trouble. Convive has disappeared.

İBADAN (I)

In the morning Mother and I will be going to Ibadan, to Convive's school. What exactly we are going to do there, I don't know. Being 'twins', Convive and I should be in the same school. But since I failed the Ibadan International School's entrance examination, and Convive passed, we had to part ways. That's how she ended up in the International School and I ended up at St Gregory's.

Of course, I didn't fail because I was dumb/dim. I failed simply because:

1. The latest version of *FIFA Soccer* came out the week before the entrance exam. You get what I'm trying to say.
2. During the exam I spent a lot of time rewriting the comprehension that appeared in the English paper. That comprehension was awfully written, and could do with major rework. (By the way, English is my best, *best* subject.) By the time I was done rewriting it was almost 'game over'. But at least I had accomplished something.

3. Stomach trouble. I like to call it Engine Trouble. I spent half of the maths paper attending to this.

All through the night I thought I heard Mother sobbing. Before I went to bed she simply announced, in an unhappy voice, that I should wake up early the next morning since I would be accompanying her to Ibadan.

Ìbadan (2)

The outstanding feature of the trip to Ibadan is the silence. SILENCE. I sit beside Martins, the driver, watching the speedometer to make a mental note of the speeds at which he changes the gears. Mother sits at the back, lost in a world of her own. Beside her is Pastor Olatoye, reading a giant Bible, his lips moving in permanent prayer. I cannot but envy his ability to spend so much time praying and reading the Bible, and thinking good thoughts and doing good deeds. And fasting.

I feel an urge to smoke that is increasing by the second. I am fighting it like a terrorist fighting the desire to terrorise. I do not *like* to smoke, but I still do it. I started because it was cool to do, but now do it because it helps me to handle stress. Or does it? Of course I've heard about lung cancer and all of that. Which is why I'm now trying to stop smoking. I heard of the chain-smoking grandfather who lived to be 104 years old, and then coughed for four days after he was dead. I appreciate the living long part of it, but not the coughing part.

I am busy thinking about all of this, when I fall asleep.

İBADAп (3)

I don't stir until we are bumping over the gravel driveway into the International School within the grounds of the University of Ibadan. If I hadn't been such a blockhead-cum-juvenile-delinquent, I'd be here too.

The school is on lunch break, so we weave slowly through crowds of boys and girls strolling leisurely, clutching food – bottles, pastries and biscuits. They seem oblivious to the presence of our car, and Martins actually has to hoot his way through. They flow out of the way without even looking at what is causing them to move. There's something zombie-like about their demeanour, the kind of nonchalance borne out of arrogance.

'The Admin block,' Mother tells Martins. 'Go on straight and turn left... yes, that building.'

I decide to spend the next few seconds looking out for pretty girls. I may be hopeless with girls, but at least I can gain expertise in staring. Truth is, I really don't give a damn about them. As far as I'm concerned, they're noisy, scheming, and perpetually moody brats. No offence meant.

The principal's office is small and loaded with books, files, photos and trophies. She is a short, fat lady with a twinkle in her eye and a low cut on her head. She speaks in a cool English accent. And she makes us feel very much at ease.

'Good morning, you're very welcome to ISI,' she says, offering us her hand one after the other. She presses a buzzer to summon someone to get more chairs. I am fascinated by the photos that cover the walls – it is interesting to see how the photos of white ex-principals give way to black, and how Anglican clergy give way to civilians.

'I'm not sure it's fair of me to say that I understand your hurt and pain,' she begins. 'Convive was – is – one of the most outstanding students who has ever passed through this school. Which explains why it was an easy decision to make her headgirl.'

She pauses to allow us to take this in.

'So it was a huge shock for me when I learnt that she was nowhere to be found. The last time anyone saw her was at breakfast on Tuesday. She didn't show up in class and, naturally, all the teachers who taught her class that day noticed. No one seemed to know where she might be. There are times when she's out representing the school at one event or the other, but this wasn't the case. The alternative was that she was in the sick bay or the hostel. She was in neither.

Which was when we began to get really worried.'

'Had anyone noticed her behaving strangely before this time?' Pastor Olatoye asks.

'Not that I know of. I mean, she's usually upbeat and always busy with one thing or the other, so it should have been easy to notice that something was wrong. No one gave me that impression. And of course her phone was switched off.'

Mother simply sits, still not saying anything. She must be willing herself to believe that she isn't imagining things. Mrs Vaughan offers us tea and biscuits. Everyone declines.

'So where does the email come in?' asks Pastor Olatoye.

'Yes, I was coming to that,' Mrs Vaughan replies. 'A friend of Convive's received a text message from her asking her to check her email immediately. Here is the email.'

She picks up a sheet of paper from her desk and hands it to Pastor Olatoye. Mother and I lean over to look at it.

From: convive2000@justice.com
To: beyoncebaby007@celebrity.com
Subject: None
dear f, pls this is between me n u. i fnk am pregnant, don't knw, very confused and disbelieving. av left

school, gone far away, to do somefn about it. my mother will die of a broken heart. i cant believe it. PLEASE DON'T SHOW ANYBODY THIS EMAIL. PLEASE PLEASE IN THE NAME OF GOD. *Find something else to tell them. Anything. Or just don't say anything. c*

Mother starts to cry. Mrs Vaughan and Pastor Olatoye try to comfort her.

'So it's true. My baby. Pregnant...'

'I'm so sorry,' says Mrs Vaughan.

'It shall be well in Jesus' Name,' says Pastor Olatoye.

Nothing, says Conquest.

If symptoms persist

That night we are sitting in our pastor's sitting room. Pastor Olatoye is the Superintending General Overseer and Administering Shepherd of the Appointed Gospel Church of the Holy Trinity.

If symptoms persist, please consult your pastor, is Mother's Motto.

I sit on the single sofa opposite three frustrated adults – Pastor Olatoye, his wife and Mother – facing the interrogation of my life.

I can see the pastor staring into the dark corners of my entire soul, his righteous spirit vexed by the hustle and bustle of the seven cardinal sins, each of which is in the middle of constructing an HQ in my mind. I can see him flinching at the dirty thoughts that flit like lightning through me at regular intervals. I see his spirit choked by the ancient smell of nicotine that clothes my spirit.

'Did your sister have a boyfriend?'

'I don't know.'

'Are you sure?'

'Yes.'

'You need to tell me the truth.'

'I am.'

'What do you know about her that you haven't told us?'

Stupid question. 'Nothing.'

'Are you sure?'

'Yes.'

'Do you know where she is?'

(Stupid question number two.)

'Where do you think she might be?'

'I don't know.'

'Are you sure?'

'Yes.'

'Tell us the truth.'

What truth? 'I don't know. Convive and I don't talk much.' I avoided Mother's eyes as I said this.

'Isn't she your sister?'

'Yes.'

'So why is there no love between you?'

'I don't know. We are different people.'

On and on we go. I imagine a host of angels fluttering around the pastor's head, teaching him what to ask, showing him grainy videos of my evil life. My life in God's *You Tube*.

I am used to this already; when I was younger it was a regular occurrence – Mother taking me to pastors to pray for me that God would save me from myself. One pastor concluded that it must have had to do with ancestral curses... that flowed down the line of my family – whoever they were.

But it had been a while since I had been taken to a pastor. So this brought back memories. Age had mellowed my usual defiance – I had once bitten a pastor who was trying to force my mouth open so the devils of delinquency could file out. Of course I wasn't the one who bit him – it was the devil!

P is for Pregnant

'P' is for many things. 'P' is for Peace. Prosperity. Progress. Palace. Pleasant. Portmanteau. Possibility. Pragmatic. Possession. All nice, beautiful, appealing, sweet-on-the-tongue words.

But 'P' is also for 'Pregnant'.

My brilliant, scholarship-amassing, bright-future, hope-of-tomorrow sister is pregnant. It must be a dream.

If it had been Conquest getting a girl pregnant, then it would not be a dream. But Convive getting pregnant is the kind of dream that one only has after a very busy day.

'Why is this happening?' Mother keeps saying, to no one in particular. Her eyes are red and swollen from too little sleep and too much crying.

I don't know what to say. I have already failed her enough. I wonder why the misfortune did not restrict itself to me, the already hopeless one? I'm quite sure that if men could get pregnant, Mother would have preferred that I be the one to have got myself pregnant.

I can hear Mother sobbing in the sitting room,

dialling Convive's number at intervals of seconds, hoping that the automated voice of the voicemail will morph into Convive's.

There is nothing anyone can do but wait. Pastor Olatoye says we should not inform the police. It is not their business. We do not want to blow things out of control. Which, of course, is dumb thinking. Doesn't it occur to him that Convive's school would have told the police?

CLUES

Mother has called all the places she imagines would come tops on Convive's 'List of Places to Run to': her godmother's; her Fulani pen-pal in Kaduna; the British Council in Abuja (she won a BC competition once, and was fêted by the Council); the Orphanage.

No one has seen her.

What this means is that my Investigations List is still blank. It's my private document, I'm not telling anyone about it. I created it to track progress in the course of investigations. It looks something like this:

Who: (Who is the father of Convive's baby?)
Why: (Why did Convive allow him?)
When: (When did the act take place?)
Where:
How:

Not a single clue.

The Adventures of Sergeant Dust

The police are the next to dig their big noses into the matter. For three days in a row they visit us at home, eyeing me like I am a prime suspect in the disappearance. The policeman I hate the most is the one I have chosen to name Sergeant Dust. Even his moustache seems to be dusty. He sits on the sofa chewing the butt of a baton, his fingers fiddling absentmindedly with his teargas case. I wonder what he is doing with teargas on a domestic investigation.

He kept asking the same questions over and over again. Mother gradually gave up hope in his ability to be of *any* help. She prefers to spend her days gazing absent-mindedly or sobbing. And, of course, amassing a huge bill making phone calls in search of my sister.

As for me, suddenly I am worried about Convive's safety. I hate to imagine that she is hurt or in pain somewhere, far away from home. Even though we are enemies, I don't think I'm heartless. I'm not. Believe me.

Abeokuta (1)

And then I get a brainwave. Fiam! Just like that. I kick myself for not thinking if it before now. I should start my investigations in Convive's room. Perhaps I'd find a clue.

Everything in her room is neatly arranged, as always. No dirty clothes, no stray items. Even the cobwebs all seem to have relocated to my room. Most of the drawers are locked. But now I have plenty of justification for experimenting with my lock-opening skills. Everything comes in handy for the neophyte criminal – knives, bottle openers, six-inch nails, broken keys, flaming candles, palm oil...

In what would count as Conquest's first major success in a long while, I open two out of five drawers. I cannot believe my luck – or rather my skill. I've always been tool-challenged, and didn't imagine that I'd make any headway with this particular task. Two out of five is not too bad, is it?

One of the drawers holds nothing of value – buttons, old notebooks, a tin of biscuits gone soft, some underwear. The other drawer promises to be more helpful. It contains what seems to be more recent stuff—Convive's archive of diaries.

Now I wouldn't advise anyone to go about looking into other people's diaries, certainly not your sister's, but in this case, circumstances demand that I ignore the laws of decorum and act for the sake of greater good. Which is what justifies my invasion of my sister's privacy.

Much of the content of the diaries is serious stuff. Convive has always been a mostly serious girl. Bent on growing up to change the world. So it dawns on me that I have to pay attention to the serious stuff if I want any clues. And then I ask myself, what clues? And, how do I know a clue is a clue. I hobble down memory lane to the days when I read Enid Blyton's mystery offerings—Famous Five, Secret Seven, the Five Find-Outers, and wish I could enlist them.

One thing keeps leaping out at me from the jumble of notes and lists. I don't know why it keeps catching my attention. All I know is that it is as though there is an invisible billboard above it screaming CLUE! I read it over and over again. It's not a very remarkable piece of information. There is a LIST OF PLACES I'D LIKE TO VISIT:

Rome
*Olumo Rock

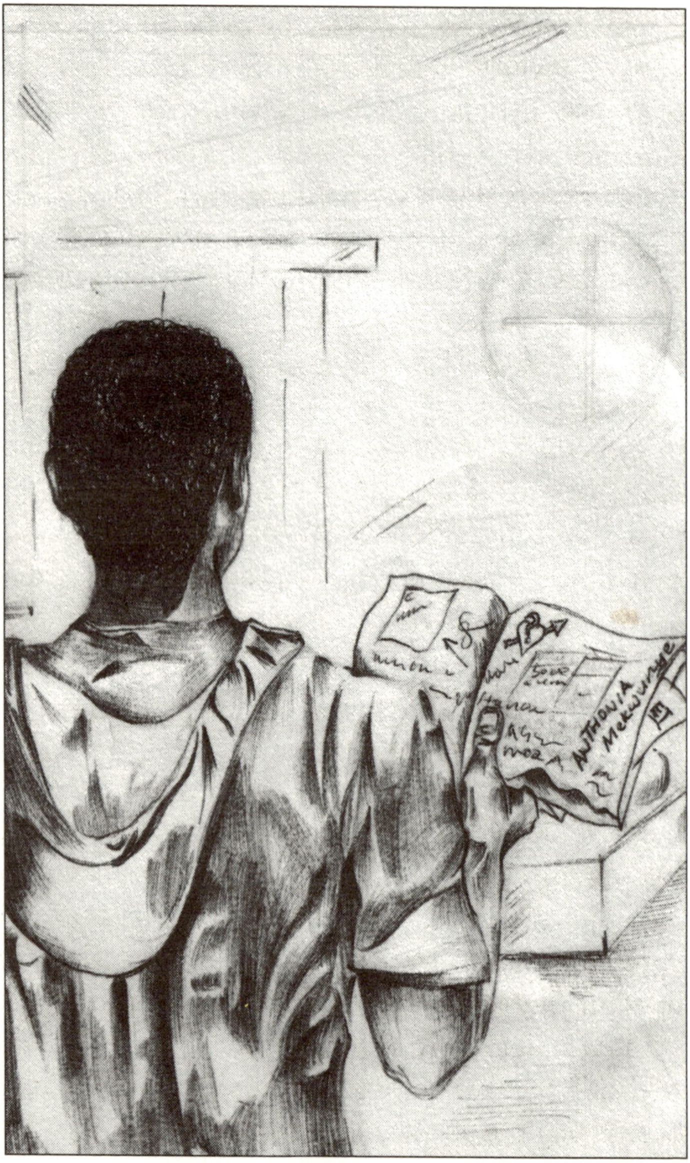
ANTHONIA
Mekwunye

Hanging Gardens
Lake Victoria
Nepal

Scrawled across that page, almost as though it were part of the list, is a name: Anthonia Mekwunye. The name looks very familiar to me, but I can't recall the connection. Then I remember; she's the popular matchmaker and youth counsellor based in Abeokuta. And 'Olumo Rock', starred in the list, is in Abeokuta. So, if I imagined that I crawled into Convive's mind, and lifted the stones there to see what lay beneath them, Abeokuta would appear more than once. Not very plausible? Well, that's how my mind works.

Abeokuta. The city under the rock. It means a lot in my scheme of things, beyond its appearance in Convive's list. My records at the orphanage give the residential address of the woman who found the abandoned Conquest as Abeokuta. (Mother told me this on my tenth birthday. In her desire to atone for the lies she had fed us from the time we could understand words, she told us a lot of things that I'm not quite sure we needed to know. Just yet.) Meaning of course that I was dumped there. Meaning that whoever gave birth to me must have been living there. Meaning that...

The leaving

At night I dream that I have found my real family. In Abeokuta. In the morning I tell Mother I am going there. I lie to her about a friend of mine (didn't she know I had no friends?) who said he had spotted Convive somewhere in Abeokuta.

'I shall have to inform the police about this,' she announces. Sergeant Dust? I can't have her tell him anything about Abeokuta. He's certainly going to find out I'm just making things up.

'No. Don't. Don't call the police. I think I can find her on my own. We don't need to get the police involved.'

'So you think it makes sense to head for a town you've never been to, just like that...'

'Yes. There's no harm in trying.'

'What if your sister isn't there?'

'Then I'll come back.'

'And who will you be staying with while you look for her?'

'With the guy who said he saw her.' It is a lie. I don't have any classmates living in Abeokuta.

'So it's absolutely normal for a mother to give her 15-year-old son money to travel 160 kilometres to a town he's never been to, in search of his missing sister?'

I don't answer. My mind is made up. I am going to Abeokuta. And I am going because of myself, and not just because of Convive.

Abeokuta (2)

This is my first successful running away from home. Of course I have always imagined that I would, and actually did pack a bag a time or two, but this is the first time my plan has come to what I'd call a logical conclusion.

I have never been to this city, but it is only a couple of hours from Lagos. I have heard a great deal about Olumo, the sprawling rock formation that overlooks the city, and from which it gets its name – Abeokuta means: 'Under Stone'.

Usually I am to be found sleeping on all those journeys that exceed an hour. But in this case, the determination with which I left home had sort of tampered with my hormones, and made sure that 'alert juices' were pumping wildly in my blood.

In the bus I sit next to an old woman who speaks in a school principal's accent and seems bent on carrying on a conversation during the entire journey. Not even when I pretend to be dozing does she catch the hint.

'You look like my grandson, boy.'

I pretend I didn't hear her. Why do I always resemble strangers? Why do people always have to walk up to me to tell me I look like someone they know? The woman pokes me in the ribs. I turn and conjure a mini-glare on my face. She doesn't see that. Yet she can see the resemblance to her grandson.

'What's your name?'

'Dave.'

'Dave? Amazing! My grandson is David. Dave. David.'

I curse my luck. Why had I chosen David? Now I not only look like her grandson, I have his name too.

'How old are you?'

'I am 17.'

'David and his twin are only 14.'

More twins!

There was no stopping her now. 'They've just got a baby brother, and I've been with them for two months in Lagos babysitting. That's what grandmas are for. Babysitting. Now I'm on my way back home to Abeokuta. I deserve some rest don't you think?'

This is when I shut my eyes and pretend I am dozing.

'So what are you going to do in Abeokuta?'

Does she actually expect that I am going to announce my mission to Abeokuta to a bus that is full of strangers? Hell no!

'Um, I'm just going, that's all.'

'I know, boy. I know you're going. What I want to know is what you're going to do there. Is it home?'

'Kind of. We lived there many years ago, before we moved to, um, Sierra Leone.'

'I can't believe this. What another coincidence. My mother is from Sierra Leone. I actually went to College there, you know!'

Oh dear! Now I've blown it big time. I have to rescue myself quick! 'Well, we actually didn't spend too long in Sierra Leone. We moved to Ghana almost immediately.'

'I see. Ghana. Lovely country. And to imagine that Ghanaians came here in droves at one time in search of greener pastures. So what brings you to Nigeria, and to Abeokuta?'

This lady is not going to let me be. I think I know her type – old, but with brains and wit working overtime.

So I fall into a 'coughing fit' – harsh, sustained coughing and welling of tears in the eyes.

She thumps me on the back, then reaches into her bag and brings out a bottle of pills.

'Here, chew this.'

Doesn't this woman realise that she is a stranger. And that even a newborn knows that no one takes anything from strangers.

'I don't take drugs.'

I am expecting the equivalent of a subpoena requesting me to explain and defend the statement I have just made. But she simply shrugs her shoulders, and puts the bottle back into her bag.

'So where did you say that you'll be staying in Abeokuta?'

'I don't know. My aunt will be picking me up at the bus station.'

I am inclined to start coughing again. Then her phone rings and she launches into a loud conversation – make that a monologue – on pensioners and the failure of the Nigerian government.

By the time she is done I have escaped into 'sleep'. I even manage to snore for effect.

Pretend-sleep eventually morphs into real sleep. I dream that I am the one who is pregnant, and that the baby growing inside me is an alien. Ugh! Then a huge hairy hand bears down on me and begins to punch my stomach. I wake up to find the old woman tapping me.

'We are in Abeokuta already. If you don't wake up now you might find yourself back in Lagos with the bus.' She cackles. 'Listen, you should ask your aunt for permission and come to visit and enjoy some home-made biscuits. You kids of nowadays, no one gives you home-made stuff any more. Here, take my number...'

I yawn, rub my eyes and stretch hard. Then it occurs to me she might be a witch or child-kidnapper. That's what they do – make little children feel at ease and then hypnotise them. If she thinks I'm easy meat for her, how wrong she is. I store her number on my phone as MA PEST although she tells me – more than once – that her name is actually Mrs George. I need to get away from her as soon as I can. I can't afford to let her know there is no 'auntie' waiting for me anywhere.

Success Motel

That night I sleep in a cheap guest-house that I find in an area called Ita-Eko. Success Motel it is called. Sadly the success does not extend to cleanliness or to freely flowing water. The manager – if I may call him that – eyes me suspiciously. The suspicion changes to faint irritation when he sees the wad of money that I pull out of my pocket.

'Na only deluxe room dey available,' he informs me. This was a man who only moments before had told me that he wasn't sure they had any rooms available. Now it's the most expensive ones that are available. Cool. I pay for only one night.

I stay awake all night killing mosquitoes and plotting my movements for the next day.

I take my bath in a tub stained a deep brown, and rush out without even eating the 'free' breakfast that I am supposed to be entitled to. One look at the burnt omelette and dry bread and I lose my appetite.

Abeokuta is a breath of fresh air. The Lagos traffic I have grown so used to is absent. I pull out the piece of paper where I have written the two most important addresses in the whole wide world: the address of the woman who found me (41, Omo Alagbede Street, off Quarry Road); and the address of the Mekwunye woman (Plot 121, Commodore Adeleke Close, Ibara Housing Estate).

I switch my phone on; it has been off since I got into town. A text message has come in from Mother: COME BACK HOME. WE HAVE HEARD FROM CONVIVE. SHE IS IN OSHOGBO. I AM ON MY WAY THERE. I am crestfallen beyond words. My journey to Abeokuta is wasted. I will have to return to Lagos with my tail between my legs.

What could Convive be doing in Oshogbo? Who does she know there? I am immersed in these thoughts, not realising that I have stepped onto the main road.

A speeding bike veers off the road, trying to avoid a car. The last thing I see is a panicked face and flailing arms on a bike out of control, headed in my direction.

Doctor, doctor

I open my eyes to find myself on a bed, surrounded by three anxious faces. I try to stand up. My right leg is in a cast and sharp pains shoot all over my body at every available opportunity. A nurse bends over to hold me back onto the bed. I want to speak, but nothing is forthcoming.

'You will be fine,' the nurse tells me.

'Thank God,' says the man on my right, smiling. 'He's come round!'

I am wondering what I am doing there. Then I remember the bike. Did it actually hit me? Damn. I hate hospitals. It's bad enough lying helplessly and being fussed over, and even worse when it's strangers who are fussing over you.

I feel like a character out of a rubbish Nigerian movie. One of my hobbies is to look out for hospital scenes in Nigerian home videos. There's no Nollywood video that doesn't have a hospital scene with a major character bandaged on the head and screaming for a nurse who is screaming for a doctor.

I feel my head. No bandage. Thank goodness. And I'm not screaming for a nurse or a doctor.

'Get me out of here,' is what comes out of my mouth.

'You're going to be fine,' the nurse tells me. 'Yes, you will be able to leave for home soon – tomorrow maybe. But you have broken your leg, I'm afraid. And you won't be able to go on your own. Where do you live? Where are your parents? We need to get in touch with them, to let them know where you are.'

I tell them that I am in town to visit with my great aunt. Without thinking, and without skipping a beat, I tell them her name. The name I tell them is the name of the woman I met in the bus on the way here: Mrs George.

And it's only then that I begin to realise the implications of the huge white plaster cast on my leg.

'You idiot!' is what Mrs George tells me when she arrives. 'Fancy lying to me that you're here to visit your aunt.' She pulls my ears hard. 'Naughty naughty runaway boy! You children of nowadays are something else.'

I confessed to her over the phone. I am ashamed of myself. No, I am not. Shame is not something I am familiar with. But I am relieved in a way that I cannot express.

'Now see what you have got yourself into. A broken leg, and God knows what else. But you should learn your lesson. No child should ever run away from home.'

I remain silent. What can I say?

She continues. 'Now I am going to make you call your folks yourself – this *minute* – and tell them the mess you're in. And apologise to them for running away from home.'

That's impossible, I think. Me, apologise? Never. Conquest does not apologise for anything. That is why he is Conquest. And that is why he got suspended from school. Because he wasn't going to grovel at anyone's feet, seeking forgiveness. To hell with the world, is the Conquest Motto.

But apologise is what I did. I couldn't believe it. I called Mother on Mrs George's phone, stammering like mad. Told her I was on a hospital bed, hit by an *okada*.

'I said apologise to her!' Mrs George hollered, slapping my shoulder. For the first time in my life I was scared of someone. And that someone was a woman. I couldn't believe it.

I heard myself telling Mother that I was sorry. I heard Mother crying. I heard her say something about her world falling apart. For the first time in a long time, I felt sad. After I finished speaking with

Mother, Mrs George collected the phone from me. She and mother spent the next 20 minutes talking. I could hear Mother sobbing over the phone. God knows what she was telling Mrs George.

Urgent Assignment

I am done for. Mrs George labels me a 'terrorist' and an 'Urgent Assignment', and proceeds to tell me tales from her days as principal of Loyola College, Ibadan, years ago. How she met kids a million times worse than me, and how she had 'taken them out of hell and taken hell out of them'. She tells me of the State Governor who was her student 30 years back, who back then had been a truant of the highest order and a lover of Indian hemp. How she had taken him as an 'Urgent Assignment', and kicked the spirit of truancy and *Igbo* out of his system. How he had written a letter to her years later to thank her for not allowing him to become a failure.

'By the time I am done with you . . .' she begins. But she does not bother to complete the sentence. She leaves me to fill in the gap. I find myself thinking about the kind of letter I would write to Mrs George in the future.

Dear Mrs George,
Sorry. This time you failed.
Yours Irredeemably,
C.

Mrs George has told Mother not to worry about me, that I am fine in her hands. To say I am shocked is an understatement. Here's a woman who doesn't know me from Adam or the Big Bang, caring for me like she gave birth to me.

And then it occurs to me: perhaps she is my real mother. And then I realise I am not thinking straight. Perhaps the accident has shifted my brain from its socket. How could she be my birth mother?

Over the next few days I find myself thinking more and more about my origins, the origins of my life – which my mother might be.

When I am discharged Mrs George takes me to her house. Life there is a military camp – at least for me. Mrs George isn't joking about redeeming me. First thing she gives me is a reading list, full of biographies of people like Mother Theresa and Mahatma Ghandi and the like.

Here's what a day in the life of Conquest looked like before I came to Abeokuta:

8–11: Mid-morning nap.
11–12: Breakfast (Mother would have left home by this time.)
12–1: Smoking (I was on ten sticks a day before I came to Abeokuta.)
1–4: TV (movies, soccer videos, Channel O).

5: Mother arrives from work. Conquest retires into oblivion/anonymity.
6–9: Lying on my bed doing nothing, just staring at the ceiling or punching a pillow.
9–11: Same as above, more or less. I pace around the room under the weight of painful boredom.

And here's what it looks like now, in Mrs George's house:

5: House alarm goes off (It is a crazy alarm; it crawls into the inner ear and explodes endlessly. Mrs George says she inherited it from her grandfather, who bought it from a Greek Sailor in Calabar in the nineteenth century. History.)
5–6: Morning devotion. Mrs George tells me that I have no choice, that when she is done with me I will know that there is a God in heaven. I've learnt not to doubt her.
6–7: House cleaning. Light duties, because of my leg, but that's no reason, Mrs George says, why I can't be useful. I have to dust every single piece of chinaware in the sitting room (and that house is a museum of chinaware). I have started to dream of myself as a bull in a china

shop. And then Mrs George always appears in the dream as a hunter wielding a rocket-propelled grenade and looking for stubborn bulls to blow off the face of the planet.

Still no breakfast yet.

7–8: I have to finish a number of assigned readings. You should see the stuff I sometimes have to read. *Gulliver's Travels* and *Robinson Crusoe* in the original ancient-English versions, one Shakespeare play per day, essays with titles like, 'Those who walk away from Omelas', 'How much land does a man need?', 'On Crime and Prejudice', etc. I've never seen such an ancient library in all of my life. No Harry Potter, no comics, no James Hadley Chase, no Michael Crichton. Now even Uncle Barnard's crappy law book has started to look like fun to me.

8–9: Vegetarian breakfast. Mrs George is a vegetarian. And she has decided I must become one too. I suffered some severe psychological reactions the first two weeks of a meat-less life. Spinach, spinach, spinach. Beans, pasta, fruit. More spinach.

9–6: Home schooling is what Mrs George calls it. It feels like school. She tutors me in physics, maths, further maths, economics and biology.

Mrs George is smarter than a genius. And look how old she is? She flits competently from subject to subject like someone changing TV channels. Vegetarian lunch somewhere in the middle.

No smoking. No dirty magazines. No time to think about how I will ruin my future.

The almost-leaving

To say I haven't been toying with the idea of running away from here is a lie. But Mrs George is the kind of person who you know can see right into your soul. Not long after I got back from the hospital, she looked at me and said, out of the blue: 'We're going to cast that spirit of smoking out.'

Yes, that's how she said it. Just like that. Who told her I smoked? Even Mother does not know. It's not something I do in public, I tried looking at her with the 'you-don't-know-what-you-talking-about' glare, but she simply shrugged her shoulders and threw an 'it's-written-all-over-you' look back.

Apart from the fact that I think Mrs George might read my mind, only an idiot would think of running away dragging something (a leg for that matter) encased in cement.

PART THREE

On the phone

'Mother wants me to have an abortion.'

This is Convive, talking to me. On the phone. Out of the blue. At 2.00 a.m.

I don't know what to say. Why is she telling me? It's her business, isn't it? She got herself into this, and she has to get herself out of it.

But I can't make myself say that to her. 'What do *you* want to do?' I ask instead.

She is quiet.

We stay silent for what seems like hours. I can hear her breathing at the other end of the phone. What is she thinking? I remember my dream about being pregnant with an alien. Has she had that dream too? I don't ask her.

'So what do you want to do?' I repeat.

She still remains silent. Then I hear what sounds like sniffing.

'I don't know,' she finally says.

'You have to make up your mind.' I wish I didn't have to find myself in this position, sounding like Convive's father, and sounding like a Mr Nice Brother. I am not her father – I am not even *from* her father – and I am not a Nice Guy. I do not care for anyone, and I think I would like to continue my life that way. Why is she calling me for advice?

By now she has started to sob. I don't know what to say. I am not the pregnant one, my sister is. And whether I like it or not, she *is* my sister, and only one at that – and she is pregnant, and she isn't even 16 yet.

I don't know if I can continue carrying on with the hostilities of before. These are difficult times.

'Did Mother tell you to have an abortion?'

'Yes.'

'When?'

'She's been hinting at it since I came home. And this morning she said it point-blank.'

'But what's the point? Everyone already knows. What are you going to tell people?'

'She says we will tell them I lost it.'

'Lost it?'

'Yes. Lost the baby. A miscarriage.'

I ponder over these words, not sure how to interpret them.

Convive continues, 'She wants me to return to school as soon as I can, and says a baby will spoil everything for me at this time.'

'So will it?'

'I don't know,' she replies. 'Please Conquest. I need your help.'

Those four words – *I need your help* – sounded like a foreign language to me. Convive needs Conquest's help. It's like the US turning to Iran and saying, 'We need your help!' Preposterous.

'But I can't help you Convive. I can't. We can't help ourselves. Can we?' I am already beginning to sound like someone out of a home video.

A teenage pregnancy is not the easiest burden in the world. And to imagine that it's a burden carried by someone filled with as much promise as my sister.

'You can, Conquest. You can. Please. Even if it's just this once. And then you can hate me again for the rest of your life if you want.'

I feel something... something strange. I have to remind myself that I am me, Conquest. The man who needs nobody – and who nobody thinks of as friend.

'Please!'

And I know I will help.

'Who did you do it for?'

'Do what?'

'Get pregnant.' I must sound callous saying that.

'I didn't *do it*, Conquest. I didn't. It just happened.'

'Yeah. Right. Still, who? How?'

'Those things do not matter at this moment,

Conquest. I made a mistake. It will hurt me all my life. You don't even know him. I barely do myself. We met at the summer Science Challenge. And it happened.'

'So does he have a name?

Convive was silent for a while. 'Fred,' she finally replies.

'Fred? Fred who? Is he white?'

'No.'

'So...' I begin. Then I stop. I never ask her again.

My fun prison and other stories

I spend the days in Mrs George's house lying down, doing my assigned readings. No TV. But despite my leg, I still have to do a lot of housework. Of course there's no smoking, no 'drinks', if you get what I mean. And there's also plenty of time to think.

To think about Convive. Think about my life. Think about that unknown family somewhere out there – one that I belong to. With my leg in a cast I cannot even leave the house in search of the address I have.

The next time Convive calls me, she is frantic. Mother has booked her an appointment with the gynaecologist. The gynaecologist is in Kaduna – far up North, the end of the world from Lagos. A very calculated way of hushing it up. And it helps greatly that there is a National Chess Competition Qualifying Game that Convive has to attend in Abuja, less than two hours drive from Kaduna. That gives a reason for travelling in the first place. Mother's plan is to have Convive participate in the competition, then travel to KD to see the doctor, undergo the abortion, and lie low in KD for a bit. Then they return to Lagos *distraught* – and say the stress of the journey had caused Convive to miscarry. And yes, while the shame of the pregnancy is something Convive would have to live with for the rest of her life, at least there would be no baby. She can start life all over again. Perhaps even return to school immediately.

We have a mother whose specialty is always getting back on her feet. Fast.

But somehow, for perhaps the first time in her life, Convive didn't want what Mother wanted for her. Of course, for me, I had *never* wanted what Mother wanted for me, which was why our relationship was *paved* with tension, all the way to the end of the road. But Convive had stayed in Mother's good books and monopolised Mother's abundance of carrots, leaving the sticks for me. Now, things had changed and the two women (for the first time I'm thinking of Convive as a woman, and not a girl) want different things.

What baffles me is why Convive doesn't want to take Mother's easy way out. Why she insists on carrying this burden the rest of her life. And then, unexpectedly, I find myself going down painful memory lane, seeing *me* as the centre of this whole drama playing – or is it replaying – itself before our eyes.

In place of my sister I see my mother, my real mother, not my adopter. She must have been about the same age as Convive when she got pregnant. I can imagine how she must have felt, stuck with a pregnancy and a future that must have looked like it was going to rain non-stop.

But she had somehow not got rid of me. Maybe she didn't *want* to get rid of me. Maybe she thought she could keep me and take care of me. Whatever happened is irrelevant. The fact is: I ENDED UP IN AN ORPHANAGE. Abandoned by the woman who gave birth to me. And adopted by a woman who was more concerned about experiments and appearances, and created artificial twins out of two people who have nothing in common. Even now it still sounds like something out of a movie.

And now, my 'sister' has become my 'mother'. And she doesn't want to go for an abortion.

Come to think of it.

If my real mother had aborted me, we wouldn't be bothering with this story. Because there would be no 'Conquest'. And perhaps a lot more people would have been happier. I would have been, for one. My school would have been, too. And even Mother. And Convive too, since we have spent quite a while living to make life miserable for each other.

A-day

Time is running out. The D-day, or shall I call it the A-day (A is for Abortion) is drawing near. I, upon whom Convive has mysteriously placed her hopes, lie bedridden in Abeokuta, 160 kilometres from Lagos, with only one functioning leg. Convive's mind is made up. She does not want the abortion.

My own mind is not even made up. I seem to like the idea of the abortion. It seems to me like a way to avoid inflicting another Conquest on an already fragile world. But...

I don't know what I am going to do.

Until I think of Mrs George.

Good news (1)

The day Convive arrives in Mrs George's house, I receive the happiest news I've had in a long, long time.

Mother has brought Convive, looking unhappy. Mother has agreed to bring her only because Mrs George has promised to speak to Convive, who by now has become quite adamant that she is not going to have an abortion.

In the last few days I have seen a resolve and determination in my sister that I have not seen in her before.

We are home alone with Mrs George, surrogate grandchildren to a woman who weeks ago had been a total stranger. Such is life.

Mother is determined to ensure that the abortion takes place. As far as I am concerned, it is her way of making everything as normal again as possible. Convive holds too much academic promise to be allowed to have a baby at 15 going on 16.

'But it's my life, isn't it?' Convive protests.

'But see where you have brought it,' Mother says, barely concealing her bitterness. Then she bursts out crying. It is how she maintains her power over Convive. Guilt. Tears. She'd begin to cry and Convive would succumb to her every wish.

Now, amazingly, Convive seems to be changing too. She looks Mother in the eyes. 'Stop it Mother! It won't work this time.' I swear I hear Mother gasp as the force of the statement hits her. She gazes at her daughter, speechless. I lie on the reclining cane chair in the room, my plastered leg laid out before me, I hide my face behind a book. Mrs George sits on a chair opposite the sofa where Mother and Convive sit. She remains silent, perhaps thinking it wise not to get too involved.

The good news I talked about. The uneasy silence that pervades the atmosphere that morning in Mrs George's house is broken by a knock on the door. It is the gateman, holding a parcel that looks like it was delivered by express mail.

'Na person jus' drop am now now...' he says, handing it over to Mrs George.

'Thank you Samson,' she says. Then, turning to me: 'It's for you.' I feel my heart thud in my chest, unable to contain my excitement. I think I know where the package is from, but I have no idea what it might contain. I received a call a week or so ago, from someone in the Lagos Ministry of Sports, asking me to give a mailing address. Since I am in

Abeokuta, and might be here for a while, I decided to use Mrs George's address.

'My letter bomb,' I joke. 'My enemies have followed me here again.'

'Silly boy,' Mrs George says, tossing the package at me. It is our attempt to lighten the load of sadness hanging upon the house.

I open the package, very gently, unlike my usual impatient self. I am already preparing myself for a huge disappointment, imagining that the package might contain a thank-you note from some 'I am directed to inform you' civil servant, and pictures that must have been taken on one football pitch or another, at one competition or another.

I am wrong.

In that package is a letter that I have only dreamt about in the wildest of my dreams. An invitation to the Lagos State Under 21 football team, in two months, when the new season begins. The letter says something about my being 'the youngest invitee' and about my 'astonishing talent', words that make me cringe with embarrassment.

Enclosed within the letter is another envelope, bearing, of all things, a cheque in my name. A cheque. I have never received a cheque before; I don't even have an account number. I have won money awards in the past, of course, for my soccer, but it has always been cash. But this is a cheque for 75 000 naira, for 'your being a member of the team that won the 2005 Lagos State Youth Soccer Championships'. Phew!

This is an achievement that I had long forgotten about. It was so long ago, and we had given up any hope of getting anything other than certificates of participation, apart from our trophy. But now, apparently, the company that sponsored the competition had dusted some files and redeemed their pledges.

Mrs George reads the letter aloud and gives me a bear hug. Something that looks like a faint smile appears on Mother's face. But maybe I am imagining things, as usual.

But. Yes, there is a *but*. Will I be able to play by the time the team starts training? Instinctively I look at Mrs George. She smiles.

'We'll talk to the physiotherapist,' she says. 'You have an appointment with her next week. She'll be able to tell you.' Then she looks like a headmistress again. 'Of course, it will take a lot of hard work and determination. You'll have to work at it!'

Convive, her eyes moist with tears, congratulates me. Then she rises from her seat and comes to hug me.

We have not hugged each other in the last God-knows-how-many years.

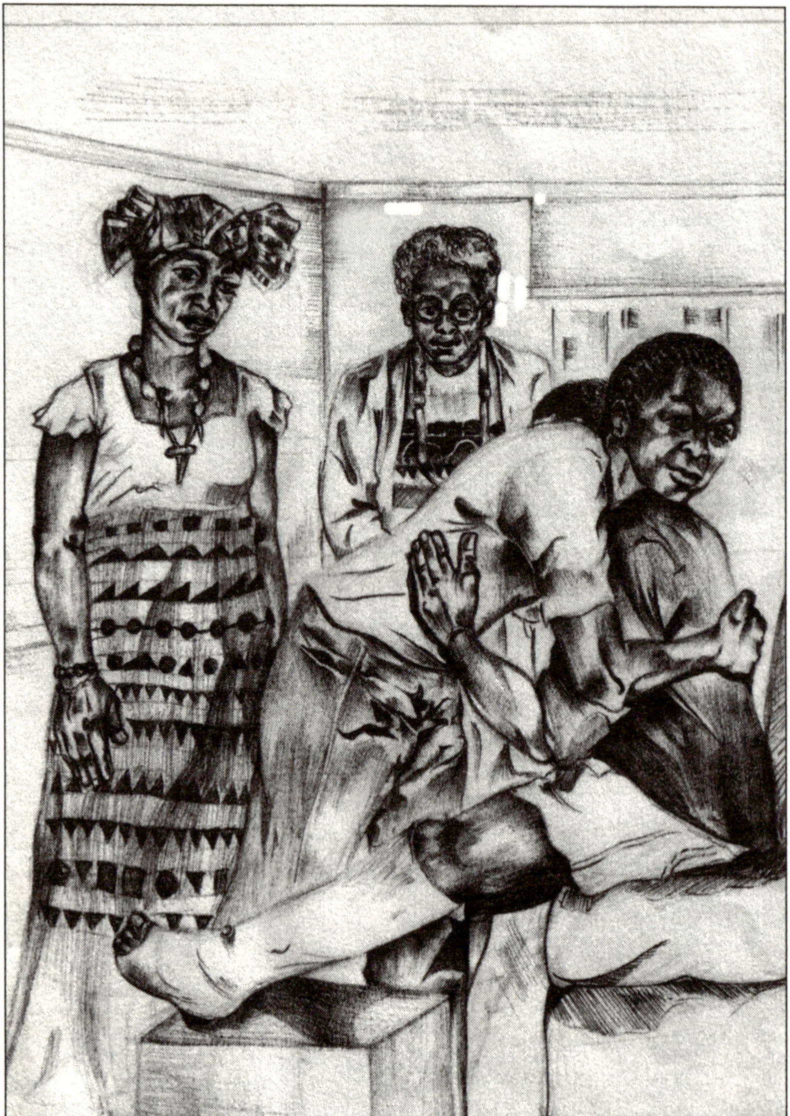

The Beginning Near the End

Mother still wants Convive to have an abortion. And time is running out. Mrs George tries to carry both parties along, to no avail. Mother keeps wondering what Convive wants to do with a baby she is obviously too young to mother. I keep getting the feeling that Mother is silently using me as an example of what the baby might turn out to be if given a chance to live.

Mrs George asks Mother to give Convive a week to think about it. Mother returns to Lagos and comes back a week later. Her mind seems made up and she has already bought tickets for the trip to Abuja, en route Kaduna.

Convive is still adamant. She keeps insisting that two wrongs have never, and would never, make a right. She keeps insisting on her right to give the baby in her a chance.

Things fall apart completely when she says, 'I do not want to be a murderer.'

Mother rises up, fire in her eyes.

'So I am the murderer, eh?' she screams. She flies at Convive and lashes out at her with both hands. Mrs George drags Convive away from Mother.

Convive is crying.

Mother is shouting at the top of her voice. All the pressure she seems to have been bearing since Convive got pregnant, bursts out – a raging volcano of regrets and disappointment. She yells about the folly of trying to raise other people's children as her own. I watch, silent, as Mother rants on and on. Somehow I pity her. The experiment she has spent her adult life putting together – raising a set of brilliant, almost-perfect twins to take the world by storm – is crumbling before her eyes.

And she seems to be crumbling too, as though she were made of the same stuff as her dreams and hopes.

When she is tired of anger and can no longer find the strength to scream, she tears up the tickets she has bought, right before our eyes, and proceeds to wash her hands of Convive and I. It is something I am not sure she means, something she has only said out of anger, but the pain of it will never leave our minds.

She storms out of Mrs George's house. The three of us – Convive, Mrs George and I – stand looking at her as she leaves, not sure what emotions we should be dealing with at this time. Anger? Fear? Hate? Disappointment?

Mrs George quickly tries to calm us down, excusing Mother's behaviour. But Convive and I can easily tell that even she is shocked.

She assures us Mother will be back after she has calmed down and regained her strength. 'And I am here for you,' she adds. It is those five simple words that calm my sister and I the most. 'I will be there for you.' They are very sweet. 'I will be there for you.'

Slowly, I reach into my pocket where the precious cheque is folded. Without really thinking about it, I hand it to Convive. 'Here,' my voice is saying, 'you can use this to get some of the things the baby will need.'

In that moment, almost like a bolt of light out of the sky, many things hit me smack on the brain. I see a vision of my future. It is a quick glimpse, and then it is gone, the way a television shuts off when the power supply goes. I did not see any soccer ball or hanging rope in that glimpse. But I thought I saw my sister. And it occurs to me that perhaps she is all I've got, and I am all she's got. And that perhaps we were not made to be enemies. Perhaps Mother's experiment might work, but only with our permission.

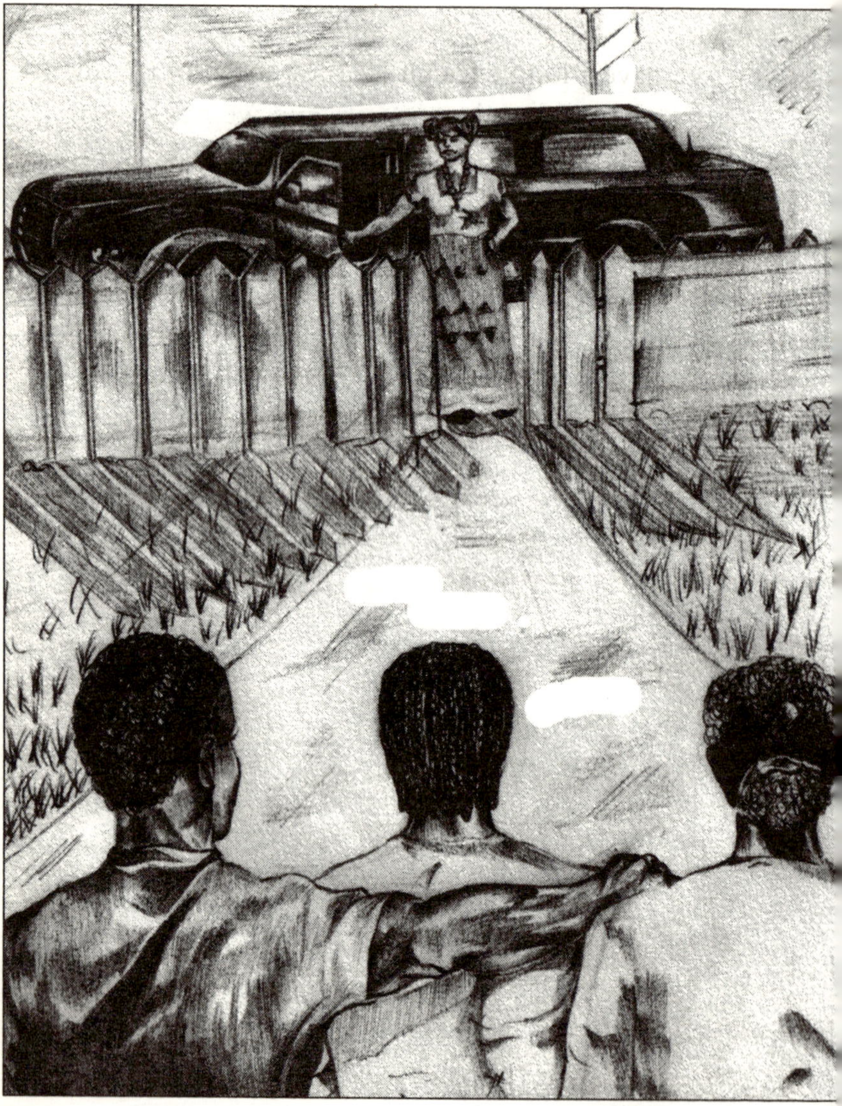

Perhaps I might be able to love my sister, no matter what happens to us in the future.

We have a long difficult journey ahead of us, my sister and I. We might triumph, and we might not. But it seems to me that we will be doubling our chances of survival if we come together on the same team. At least this once.

And one last thing. I think I also saw a glimpse of a brand new Conquest. Maybe it is possible. Mrs George tells me it is. Only time will tell.

If you enjoyed reading this story, look out for these other titles in the Hodder African Readers series...

Dear Miss Winfrey

Helen Brain

Thandeka has a dream. She wants to leave her rural school and get accepted into the Oprah Winfrey Leadership Academy for Girls. When she learns that her headmistress didn't even put forward her name for Oprah's school, she decides to take matters into her own hands and find a way to get to the school hundreds of kilometres away. The journey turns into a nightmare and Thandeka lands up in hospital trying desperately to keep her dream alive.

Shoot for the Moon

Bridget Krone

When Boipelo reads about a Canadian man who trades a red paper clip on the Internet for a house, he decides to try a similar idea in his village. He starts with a clay cow to trade and ends up with...an unexpected result.

Can he bear the embarrassment of the whole village laughing at his idea? How will he fix his relationship with his best friend? Will the girl he admires think he's an idiot? And how will he dodge the shady deals that people want him to make?

Madulo & Co.

Dabilo M. Mokobi

Madulo goes to spend her school holiday with her cousin in Serowe. She doesn't expect it to be too exciting, but thanks to an unfriendly bus driver, a teenage boy, an expedition with her friends, a frightening encounter with thieves and a certificate for bravery, the holiday turns out to be the adventure of a lifetime.

The Mystery of Rukodzi Mountain

Blessing Musariri

Simbai and Primrose come from the city to visit their grandmother and their cousin, Star, in their small village. The three cousins take a trip up the sacred Rukodzi Mountain and find themselves caught up in an adventure beyond their wildest imagination.

Simbai wants to prove to Star that there are no spirits on the mountain. Star is looking for something precious that she has lost. And Primrose wishes she had never joined them on the journey full of strange creatures and unexpected magic. The three cousins must put their differences aside and work together to find their way back down before daylight, or be lost forever.